Good thing you're not an octopus! /
E Mar   144084

Markes, Julie.
Wilton Public Library

DATE DUE

WDC			
RE			

For Charlie
—J.M.

For Johann
—M.S.

Good Thing You're Not an Octopus!
Text copyright © 2001 by Julie Markes
Illustrations copyright © 2001 by Maggie Smith
Manufactured in China. All rights reserved. No part of this book may be
used or reproduced in any manner whatsoever without written permission
except in the case of brief quotations embodied in critical articles and reviews.
For information address HarperCollins Children's Books, a division of HarperCollins Publishers,
1350 Avenue of the Americas, New York, NY 10019.
www.harperchildrens.com

Library of Congress Cataloging-in-Publication Data
Markes, Julie.
Good thing you're not an octopus! / by Julie Markes ;
pictures by Maggie Smith.   p.   cm.
Summary: A little boy finds that his life is pretty easy compared to how it might be.
ISBN-10: 0-06-028465-X. — ISBN-10: 0-06-028466-8 (lib. bdg.)
ISBN-10: 0-06-443586-5 (pbk.)
ISBN-13: 978-0-06-028465-7 — ISBN-13: 978-0-06-028466-4 (lib. bdg.)
ISBN-13: 978-0-06-443586-4 (pbk.)
[1. Animals—Fiction.   2. Self-acceptance—Fiction.]
I. Smith, Maggie, 1965–   ill.   II. Title.
III. Title: Good thing you are not an octopus.
PZ7.M339454Go   2001   99-37139   [E]—dc21

Typography by Elynn Cohen
❖

Good Thing You're Not an OCTOPUS!

Story by **Julie Markes** • Pictures by **Maggie Smith**

HarperCollins Publishers

You don't like to get dressed in the morning?

It's a good thing

you're not an octopus.

If you were an octopus,
you would have *eight* legs
to put in your pants!

You don't like to
put on your shoes?

It's a good thing

you're not a caterpillar.

If you were a caterpillar,
you would have *sixteen* feet
to put shoes on!

You don't like to ride in your car seat?

It's a good thing

you're not a kangaroo.

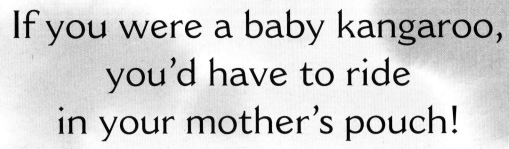

If you were a baby kangaroo,
you'd have to ride
in your mother's pouch!

You don't like
to eat your lunch?

It's a good thing

you're not a bird.

If you were a bird,
you would have to eat
worms for lunch!

Robins

You don't like
to take a nap?

It's a good thing

you're not a bear.

If you were a bear,
you would have to nap
all winter long!

You don't like to take a bath?

It's a good thing

you're not a tiger.

If you were a baby tiger,
your mother would have
to lick you clean!

You don't like to
brush your teeth?

It's a good thing

you're not a shark.

If you were a shark,
you could have *two hundred*
teeth to brush!

So, the next time you need to

get dressed,

go for a ride,

eat your lunch,

take a nap,

take a bath,

or brush your teeth,

remember:

It's a good thing you're YOU!

PHEW!

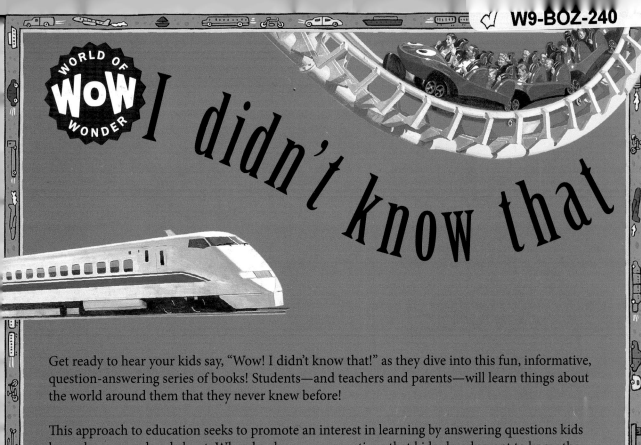

I didn't know that

Get ready to hear your kids say, "Wow! I didn't know that!" as they dive into this fun, informative, question-answering series of books! Students—and teachers and parents—will learn things about the world around them that they never knew before!

This approach to education seeks to promote an interest in learning by answering questions kids have always wondered about. When books answer questions that kids already want to know the answers to, kids love to read those books, fostering a love for reading and learning, the true keys to lifelong education.

Colorful graphics are labeled and explained to connect with visual learners, while in-depth explanations of each subject will connect with those who prefer reading or listening as their learning style.

This educational series makes learning fun through many levels of interaction. The entertaining information combined with fantastic illustrations promote learning and retention, while question and answer boxes reinforce the subject matter to promote higher order thinking.

Teachers and parents love this series because it engages young people, sparking an interest and desire in learning. It doesn't feel like work to learn about a new subject with books this interactive and interesting.

This set of books will be an addition to your home or classroom library that everyone will enjoy. And, before you know it, you too will be saying, "Wow! I didn't know that!"

"People cannot learn by having information pressed into their brains. Knowledge has to be sucked into the brain, not pushed in. First, one must create a state of mind that craves knowledge, interest, and wonder. You can teach only by creating an urge to know." - Victor Weisskopf

© 2016 Flowerpot Press

Contents under license from Aladdin Books Ltd.

Flowerpot Press
142 2nd Avenue North
Franklin, TN 37064

Flowerpot Press is a Division of Kamalu LLC, Franklin, TN, U.S.A. and
Flowerpot Children's Press, Inc., Oakville, ON, Canada.

ISBN 978-1-4867-0500-9

Designer:
Concept, editorial, and design by
David West Children's Books.

Illustrators:
Ross Watton
Jo Moore

American Edition Editor:
Johannah Gilman Paiva

American Redesign:
Jonas Fearon Bell

Copy Editor:
Kimberly Horg

Educational Consultant:
Jim Heacock

Printed in China.

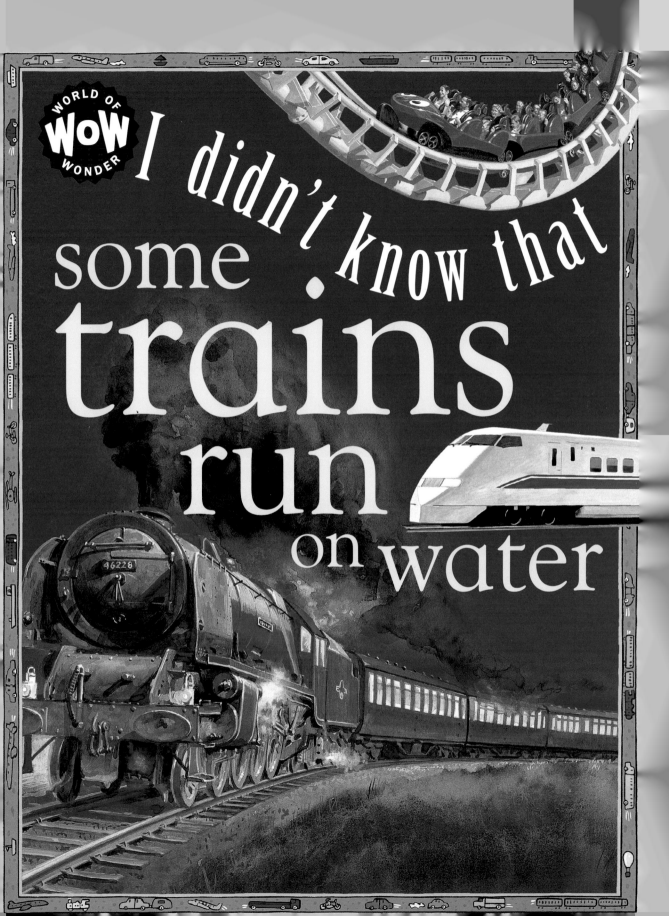

I didn't know that

Introduction

Did you know that trains opened up the American West? That the *Flying Hamburger* was a train? That trains can go upside down? Discover for yourself amazing facts about rail transportation, from the earliest steam trains that traveled at walking pace to the latest technology of the high-speed supertrains.

Watch for this symbol, which means there is a fun project for you to try.

True or false?
Watch for this symbol and try to answer the question before reading on for the answer.

I didn't know that

the first steam trains went slower than walking pace. In 1804, Richard Trevithick's steam engine pulled ten tons of iron ore and 70 passengers over 9 miles (14.5 km). It took four hours and five minutes. Trevithick walked ahead all the way.

Can you find the running boy?

In 1829, *Rocket*, built by George Stephenson, won a competition for the best steam engine. It had an average speed of 12 mph (19 km/h) and a top speed of 29 mph (about 47 km/h).

True or false?

Horses pulled the first railroad trains for passengers.

Answer: True.
Nearly 200 years ago, passengers were pulled by horses on the world's first passenger line in Wales. The Emperor and Empress of Austria used this form of transportation 25 years later (above left).

! *Catch Me Who Can gave rides to fare-paying passengers.*

I didn't know that

steam trains run on water.
A steam engine uses water to get its power.
A coal fire heats the water. The boiling water
turns to steam. The steam is forced into the
cylinders where pistons are pushed that
turn the wheels.

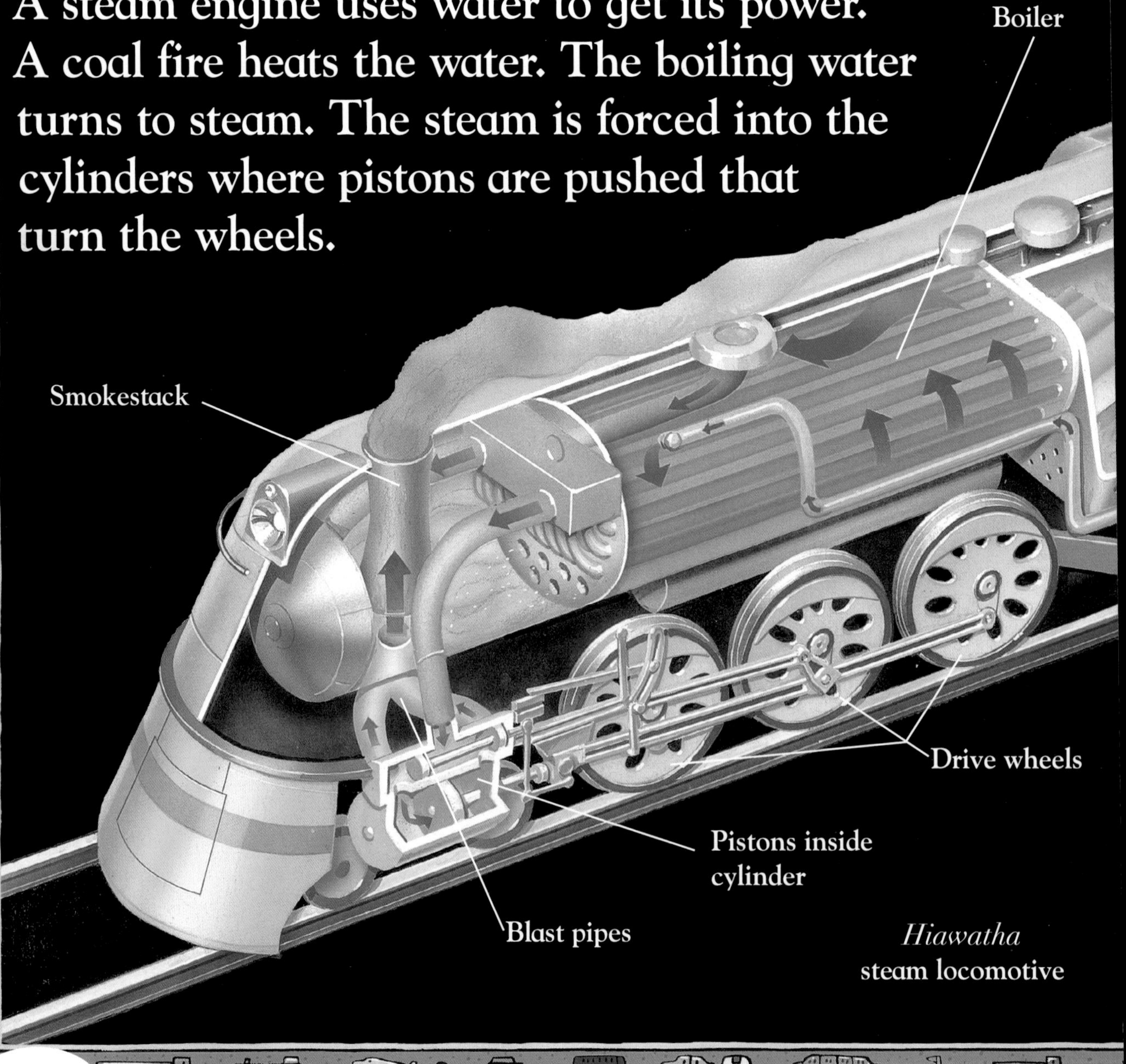

Boiler

Smokestack

Drive wheels

Pistons inside
cylinder

Blast pipes

Hiawatha
steam locomotive

Trains can't always carry enough fuel, so
on long journeys they have to stop to take
on more fuel and water.

Tender

Water

Driver

Coal

Firebox

Fireman

As well as the driver who controls the
speed, reads the signals, and stops and
starts the train, each locomotive needs a
fireman to tend the boiler. It is his job to
stoke the fire in the firebox and keep the
boiler well supplied with water.

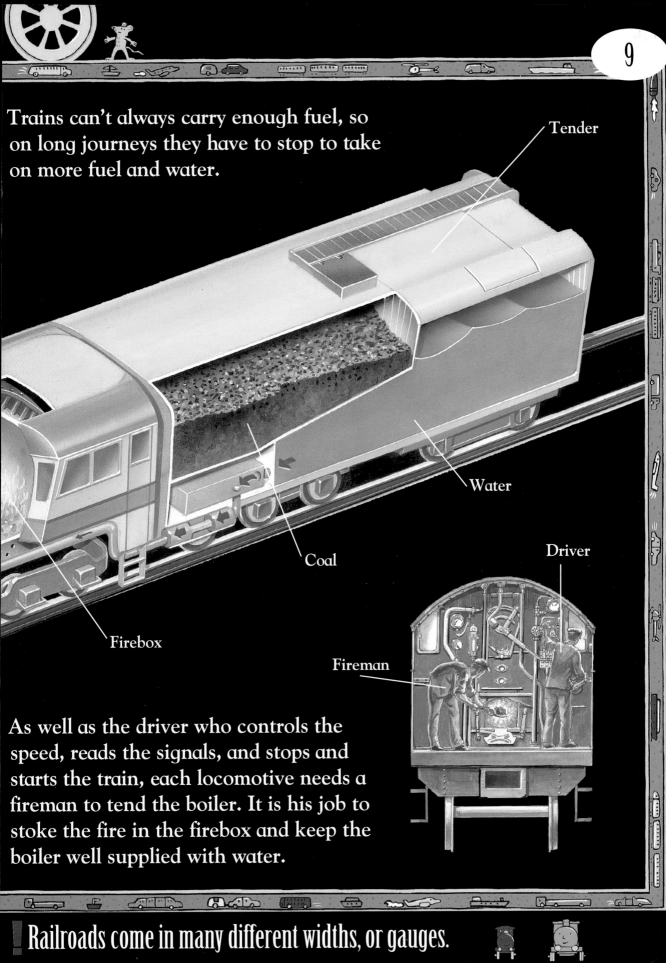

Railroads come in many different widths, or gauges.

I didn't know that

steam trains opened up the American West. By 1850, the railroad companies had bought the land and laid track from coast to coast. At last, goods could get from factories in the East to the new towns in the West.

Can you find the three train robbers?

Two teams built the Union Pacific Railroad across America, starting from opposite ends. They met in Utah in 1869.

 True or false?
Casey Jones was a famous train builder.

Answer: False.
The real Casey Jones was an engineer who died in 1900 when his engine, the *Cannonball Express*, hit a freight train that was stalled. Jones knew he couldn't slow down fast enough. He made his fireman jump to safety, and all the passengers survived.

Early railroad travelers were often attacked by robbers.

American type 4–4–0
steam locomotive

! Before steam trains, settlers traveled in wagon trains.

I didn't know that

the biggest steam locomotive had 24 wheels. *The Big Boy* hauled freight trains on the Union Pacific in the 1940s. This enormous articulated locomotive was nearly 131 feet (40 m) long.

Mallard was a famous streamlined British steam engine. It set the steam speed record of 126 mph (203 km/h) in 1938. This record has never been broken!

! One of the longest trains ever pulled 500 cars of coal!

Wheel codes are the numbers used to describe an engine's "wheel combination." The 2-6-2 on the left has 2 leading wheels, 6 driving wheels, and 2 trailing wheels. Can you figure out the wheel codes for A, B, C, and D?

2 - 6 - 2

A

B

C

D

Answers: A. 0-4-0 B. 2-6-0 C. 4-6-4 D. 2-8-2

UNION PACIFIC

4019

This is the 1866 steam locomotive *Peppersass*. It pushed cars up mountains. The wheels and rails were both "toothed" (called "rack and pinion") so they could grip each other.

9

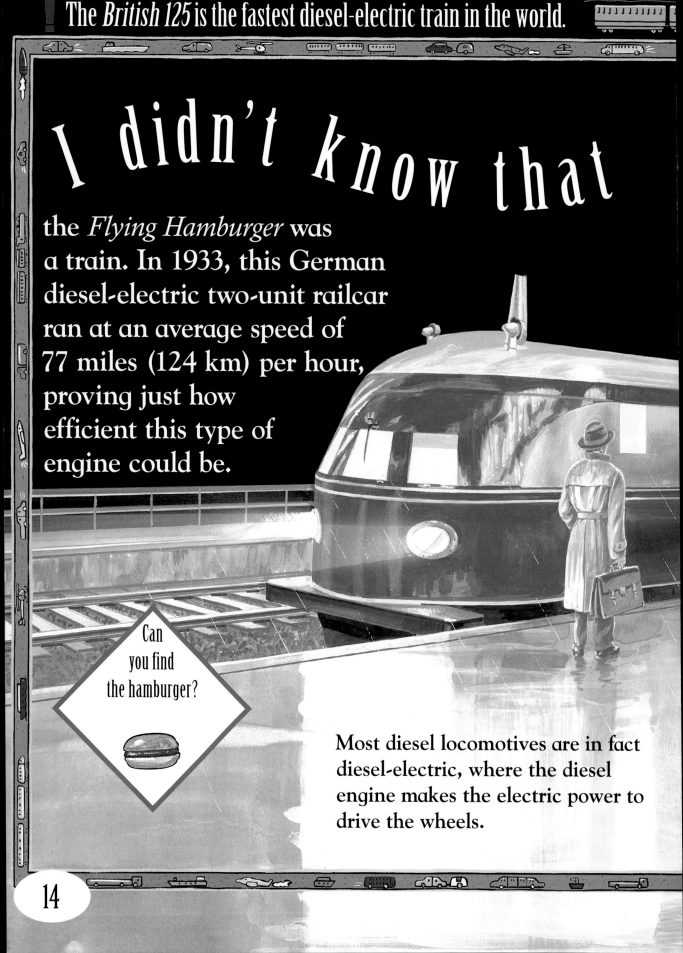

I didn't know that

the *Flying Hamburger* was a train. In 1933, this German diesel-electric two-unit railcar ran at an average speed of 77 miles (124 km) per hour, proving just how efficient this type of engine could be.

Can you find the hamburger?

Most diesel locomotives are in fact diesel-electric, where the diesel engine makes the electric power to drive the wheels.

True or false?
Some trains had propellers.

Answer: True.
A diesel engine powered the propeller at the back of the German *Kruckenburg*. It broke the world record in 1931 with an average speed of 143 miles (230 km) per hour for over 6 miles (9.5 km).

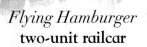

Flying Hamburger
two-unit railcar

The *Kitson-Still* of 1924 (right) was diesel driven, but the heat from the diesel engine also heated water to produce steam— for that extra push!

! Diesel trains began to be used in the United States in 1934.

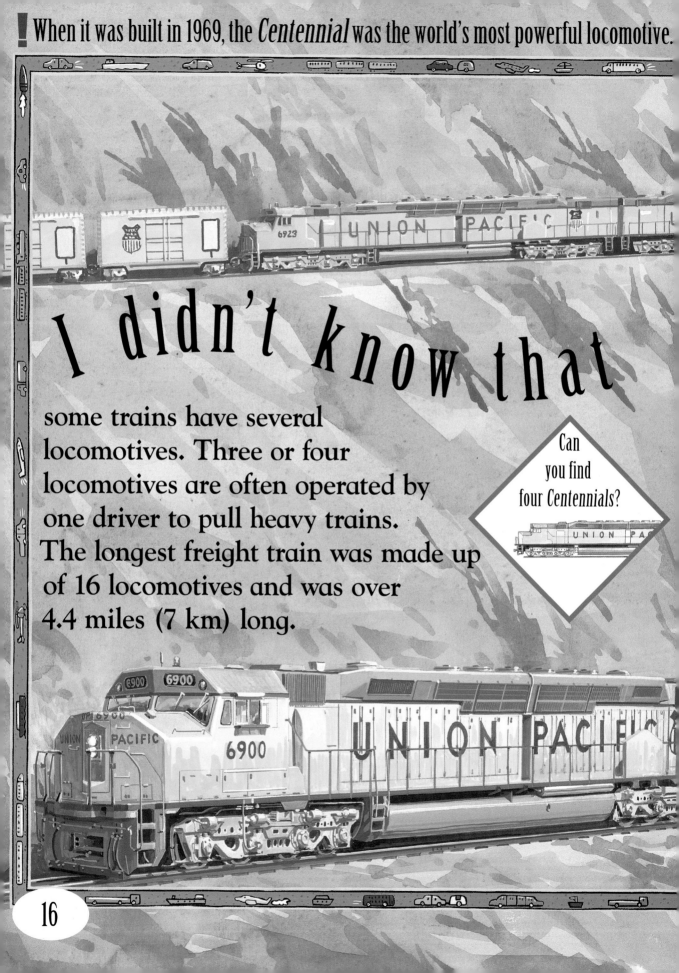

I didn't know that

some trains have several locomotives. Three or four locomotives are often operated by one driver to pull heavy trains. The longest freight train was made up of 16 locomotives and was over 4.4 miles (7 km) long.

Can you find four Centennials?

Powerful diesel-electric locomotives (below) "shunt" (push or pull) cars over short distances or in freight yards.

The individual cars of a freight train often go to separate destinations. As they pass through the classification yard, their labels are scanned from the control tower. Computerized points then send them in the right direction.

PACIFIC 6920

UNION PACIFIC 6903

Union Pacific celebrated their 100 years with their new *Centennial*. 100

I didn't know that

some trains don't make their own power. Some electric trains get their power from overhead wires via a metal pantograph on the roof, others from a conductor rail on the ground.

❗In 1883, Britain's first electric railroad ran along the seafront in

The *Regio Runners* in Holland (right) are double-decker inter-city trains, powered from overhead electric wires.

French *Class 12000* electric locomotive

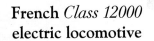

True or false?
There were electric trains more than 100 years ago.

Answer: True.
Werner von Siemens (below) gave a demonstration of his electric locomotive in Berlin in 1879.

I didn't know that

trains run beneath the city. The oldest (1863) and longest underground system is in London. Underground rail systems are now used all over the world.

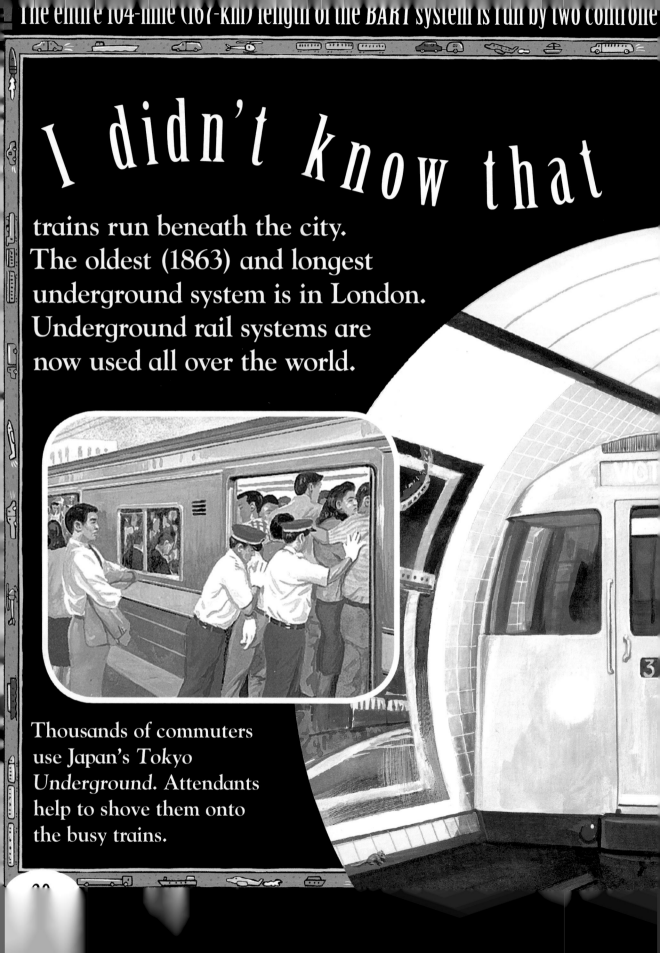

Thousands of commuters use Japan's *Tokyo Underground.* Attendants help to shove them onto the busy trains.

True or false?
Some trains don't need drivers.

Answer: True.
The *Docklands Light Railway* (*DLR*, above left) in London, and the *Bay Area Rapid Transit* system (*BART*) that runs under the San Francisco Bay are operated from control centers by computers. A supervisor travels on board the *DLR* in case anything goes wrong.

Can you find the four mice?

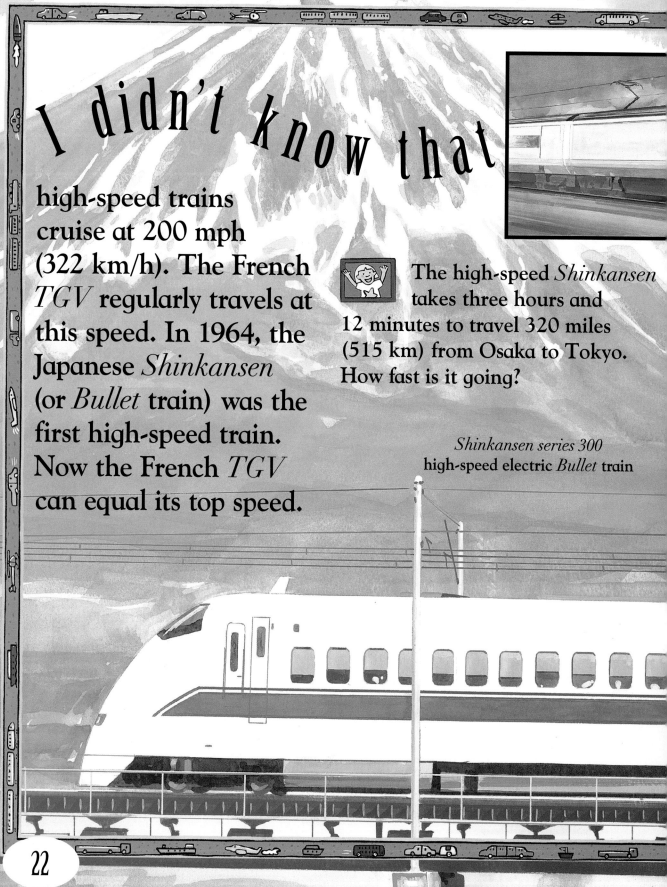

I didn't know that

high-speed trains cruise at 200 mph (322 km/h). The French *TGV* regularly travels at this speed. In 1964, the Japanese *Shinkansen* (or *Bullet* train) was the first high-speed train. Now the French *TGV* can equal its top speed.

The high-speed *Shinkansen* takes three hours and 12 minutes to travel 320 miles (515 km) from Osaka to Tokyo. How fast is it going?

Shinkansen series 300 high-speed electric Bullet train

Eurostar speeds from London to Paris in three hours. It goes under the English Channel from Folkestone to Calais in only 19 minutes. It is a British design based on the *TGV*.

True or false?
Some high-speed trains lean over when they go around corners.

Answer: True.
Trains that lean into curves, like a cyclist on a bicycle, can go faster around bends. Computers on the Italian *ETR* and the Swedish *X2000* (below) tell the train how far to lean as it goes around the bends.

I didn't know that

some trains run on only one rail. A monorail train rides either above or below a single rail. Two vertical wheels guide it along the track and horizontal wheels grip the sides. Sydney's monorail is built on stilts.

The *Ballybunion Line* in Ireland was a monorail system from 1888 to 1924. Invented by Frenchman Charles Lartigue, the double engine rode on an A-shaped line.

A train with no wheels! *TACV* stands for "tracked air cushion vehicle"– a hovercraft on rails. This experimental *Aérotrain* is powered by a jet plane's engine.

The power of electromagnets can lift a train above the tracks so that it runs without friction, like this *Maglev* train. If you experiment with two ordinary magnets, you will discover just how strong their pull (attraction) and push (repulsion) can be.

A *Maglev* in Birmingham, England

Sydney, Australia's *AEG von Roll* monorail

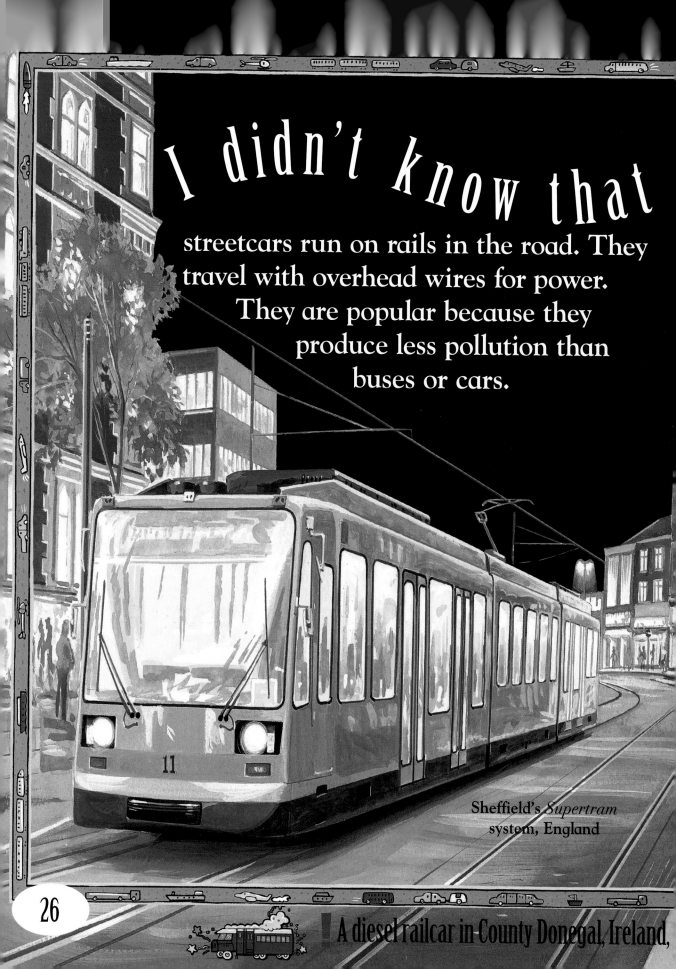

I didn't know that

streetcars run on rails in the road. They travel with overhead wires for power. They are popular because they produce less pollution than buses or cars.

Sheffield's *Supertram* system, England

A diesel railcar in County Donegal, Ireland,

Not all trains look like trains. This railcar, built in 1932 for the County Donegal Joint Railways in Ireland, looks much more like a bus!

True or false?

The cars on a cable railroad have electric engines.

Answer: False.
The famous cable cars in San Francisco are pulled along by a moving loop of steel cable. The cable runs along a slot in between the rails and the cars clamp onto it.

clocked up nearly 1 million miles (1.6 million km).

I didn't know that

some trains run upside down. Rollercoasters run on rails. They are scary, but not dangerous. Speed and gravity secure them. Many have hooks around the rails to hold them safely in place.

Have a whole rail network in your own room! Most models are replicas of full-size trains. They are usually electric.

True or false?
Some miniature trains carry passengers.

Answer: True.
You can visit real miniature railroads and even ride on some of them. This one is steam-powered and is one-fifth the size of the original it was copied from.

Glossary

Articulated
Built in connected sections.
Helps long vehicles to go
around bends more easily.

Cable railroad
A railroad where passenger
cars are pulled along by a
moving cable, operated by a
stationary motor.

Classification yard
A place where freight cars are
shunted (pushed or pulled) to
make up trains.

Computerized
Any system that is controlled
by computers.

Conductor rail
Electrified rail that passes
electricity to an electric train.

Cylinder
Sealed tube in which gas
expands to push a piston.

Diesel-electric
On diesel-electric trains
the diesel engine powers
a generator that provides
electricity for the motor.

Gauge
The distance between the two
rails on a railroad track.

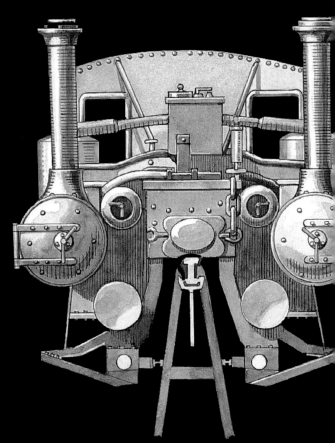

Maglev
Short for "magnetic levitation." A train that is moved along above the track by magnetism.

Monorail
Railcars that run on one rail.

Pantographs
The metal frames on top of an electric train that pick up the electric current from overhead wires.

Piston
The disk that moves inside the cylinder, attached to a rod that turns a crankshaft or flywheel.

Points
A junction where rails can be moved to send a train in a different direction.

Rack and pinion
A system of notched wheels and rails used on mountain railroads.

TACV
Tracked Air Cushion Vehicle —one that moves on a cushion of air above a track.

Wheel combination
The way in which a locomotive's leading (front), driving, and trailing (back) wheels are arranged.

Index